THIS

Young Knight

BOOK BELONGS TO

James Fox

The Big Storm

CHRISTINE PULLEIN-THOMPSON

The Big Storm

illustrated by
Lesley Smith

HODDER AND STOUGHTON

British Library Cataloguing in Publication Data
Pullein-Thompson, Christine *1930-*
  The big storm.
  I. Title   II. Smith, Lesley *1951-*
  823.914 [J]
  ISBN 0-340-53344-7

Text copyright © Christine Pullein-Thompson 1988
Illustrations copyright © Lesley Smith 1988

First published 1988 by Hodder and Stoughton Children's Books
Young Knight edition first published 1991

Published by Hodder and Stoughton Children's Books,
a division of Hodder and Stoughton Ltd,
Mill Road, Dunton Green, Sevenoaks, Kent TN13 2YA
Editorial office: 47 Bedford Square, London WC1B 3DP

Printed in Great Britain by Cambus Litho, East Kilbride

Annie woke up. It was still dark outside and her window was rattling. Martin was sitting up in bed. 'Don't worry, Annie. It's only a big storm,' he said.

Annie put on the light and they crept
downstairs. Mum was in the kitchen.
Dad was away selling tractors.

'We can't sleep. The wind's trying to get
into the house and I'm frightened,' Annie
said.

'It's all right, it woke me up too,' said Mum, giving Annie a hug.

'It's a big storm, isn't it?' asked Martin, who was six.

Annie, who was five, climbed on to a stool and looked out of the window. The big tree outside was bending and cracking. There was a faint moon hiding in a sky full of wild, dark clouds.

'I wish Dad was here too,' Annie said.

Then the big tree fell with a tremendous
crash and all the lights in the house went
out. Annie screamed. Martin shouted,
'What's happening, Mum?'

'The electricity wires must be down. Stay
where you are. I'll find a torch,' replied
Mum, feeling her way round the kitchen.

'Will the house fall down?' asked Martin.

'Of course not,' said Mum, switching on the torch. Then they heard glass breaking upstairs.

'We had better see what's happened,' Mum said.

They went upstairs slowly, as though there was a wild animal there ready to pounce.
The landing window was broken. There was glass and bits of tree on the carpet.
The wind was howling louder than ever.
It rushed triumphantly through the broken window and tied the curtains in knots.

'I don't want to go back to bed,' Annie said.

'Nor me,' agreed Martin.

So they went downstairs again.
Mum wanted a cup of tea, but the electric
kettle wasn't working, nor was the
telephone. The heating wasn't working
either. Annie looked out of the window
again. The fallen tree looked like a sleeping
giant. The sky was growing lighter. It was
nearly morning. They dressed in the kitchen
by torchlight.

Then Martin opened the back door a few centimetres and looked out. For a moment the wind was silent, and Martin could hear a strange noise coming from the end of the garden. A mewing noise! He stood listening to it, and Annie said, 'What is it, Martin? What's crying?'

But now Martin was shouting, 'There's a
cat trapped at the end of the garden,
Mum. It's hurt.' And then he was running
outside into the storm without coat, hat, or
gloves.

'Come back, Martin. Come back at once,'
cried Mum, running after him, while Annie
stood terrified on the doorstep.

The fence at the end of the garden was lying down. Electric wires lay tangled in the fallen tree. Plants had been uprooted. Broken branches were scattered across the lawn. The garden seat was upside down. And the wind was howling louder than ever.

'Mum! Martin! Come back – you'll be killed,' sobbed Annie.

Mum and Martin had reached the fallen fence.

'Help me prop it up. Quick,' Mum said.

They pushed and pushed. Then Mum
bent down and pulled out the cat. It mewed
and spat at her, but she kept saying, 'It's all
right, pussy. There's a good pussy.'

Then, holding it under one arm, she ran
to the house with Martin following. The wind
slammed the back door shut after them.

'Quick, get a cardboard box from under the stairs, and a cushion, Annie,' gasped Mum.

The cat was quieter now. Mum laid him on a cushion in the cardboard box. She put netting over the top so he couldn't get out. Then she turned to Martin. 'Never do that again, do you hear? You were a very naughty boy. You could have been killed by a falling tree,' she said.

Martin stared at the floor and said nothing. Annie looked through the netting at the cat. It was big and ginger with beautiful yellowy-green eyes.

Mum bathed the scratches the cat had made on her hands and put plasters on them. 'He was frightened, poor thing. He didn't mean to hurt me,' she said.

They ate cereal with milk for breakfast. Annie didn't finish hers. Martin didn't taste his. They were worried about the cat, and sad about the fallen tree, which they had loved. We won't be able to have tea under it ever again, Annie thought sadly.

After a time everything was very quiet —
the wind had stopped blowing. Then they
heard a peculiar noise coming from inside
the cardboard box.

'Listen, it's the cat. I think it's dying,' cried
Annie.

'It's a he, and he isn't dying, he's purring.
That means he's very, very happy,' said
Mum.

'So he's going to be all right?' asked
Annie, who wanted to be certain.

'Yes, he wouldn't be purring if he wasn't all right,' Mum said.

Then Annie jumped up and down with joy and shouted, 'Hurray! Hurray!'

Mum lifted the cat gently out of the box
and placed a bowl filled with bread and
milk in front of him. 'We can't keep him.
We must find his owner,' she said.

Annie and Martin looked at each other. They felt very sad. The cat licked the bowl clean. Then he jumped on to the table and, looking at them with his beautiful eyes, purred and purred.

'I think he's trying to say thank you,' said Mum.

Next day, when life was nearly normal again, they tried to find the cat's owner. They asked at the police station, at the corner shop, at the veterinary surgery. They even put a notice in the local paper, which said, FOUND: BIG GINGER CAT, and their address underneath.

The scratches on Mum's hands healed.
Dad returned from selling tractors.
And when he wasn't sawing up the fallen
tree, he asked everyone he met whether
they had lost a cat.

But no one ever claimed the big ginger cat with the beautiful eyes. So they called him Stormy and he lived happily with Martin and Annie for the rest of his life.